Put Beginning Readers on the Right Track with
ALL ABOARD READING™

The All Aboard Reading series is especially for beginning readers. Written by noted authors and illustrated in full color, these are books that children really and truly *want* to read—books to excite their imagination, tickle their funny bone, expand their interests, and support their feelings. With four different reading levels, All Aboard Reading lets you choose which books are most appropriate for your children and their growing abilities.

Picture Readers—for Ages 3 to 5
Picture Readers have super-simple texts with many nouns appearing as rebus pictures. At the end of each book are 24 flash cards—on one side is the rebus picture; on the other side is the written-out word.

Level 1—for Preschool through First Grade Children
Level 1 books have very few lines per page, very large type, easy words, lots of repetition, and pictures with visual "cues" to help children figure out the words on the page.

Level 2—for First Grade to Third Grade Children
Level 2 books are printed in slightly smaller type than Level 1 books. The stories are more complex, but there is still lots of repetition in the text and many pictures. The sentences are quite simple and are broken up into short lines to make reading easier.

Level 3—for Second Grade through Third Grade Children
Level 3 books have considerably lor〔 〕〔 〕nd more complicated sentences.

All Aboard for happy reading!

Adapted (loosely) by Jennifer Dussling
from the movie *Muppet Treasure Island*

Original screenplay by
Jerry Juhl & Kirk R. Thatcher
and James V. Hart

Based (very, very loosely)
on the novel by
Robert Louis Stevenson

ALL
ABOARD
READING™

Level 3
Grades 2-3

Muppet TREASURE ISLAND™

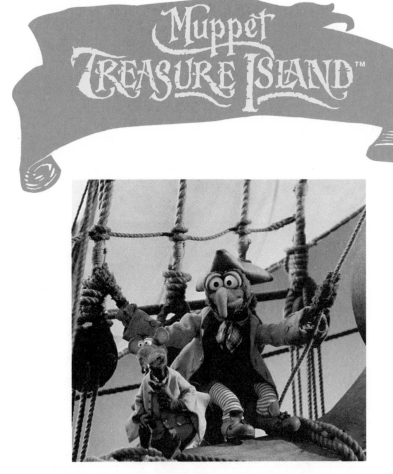

With photos from the movie
Muppet Treasure Island

MUPPET PRESS
Grosset & Dunlap • New York

The Map

It was late at night at the old inn. Billy Bones was telling a story. Rizzo, Gonzo, and Jim Hawkins groaned. They knew this story by heart. Billy told it every night. It was the story of Captain Flint and his treasure.

"...And so Flint buried the treasure on an island. He died before he could dig it up," Billy Bones went on. "To this day no one knows who has his map."

All of a sudden, Billy Bones stopped
talking. There was a noise in the yard.

Tap-tap-tap. Billy Bones turned white.

Tap-tap. The noise was coming closer.

Tap-tap-tap. It was outside the door.
The door slowly opened.

"It's Blind Pew!" Billy shrieked.

"I know you're here, Billy!" Pew said.
He took a few steps and stumbled over a
chair. Then he crashed into the wall.

Pew's hand touched an old moosehead.
"Ah, Billy," he said to the moose. "I'd
know your face anywhere!"

Billy Bones could not help it. He
laughed. That was a big mistake! Now
Blind Pew knew just where Billy was.
Pew spun around. He handed
something to Billy. Then Blind Pew
tap-tapped out the door.

Billy Bones opened his hand. There
was a piece of paper with a black circle
on it.

"The Black Spot!" Billy Bones
shouted. "The pirates are coming to…"
He dragged a finger across his throat.

"To shave him?" Rizzo asked.

"No, nitwit." Gonzo lowered his voice.
"To kill him!"

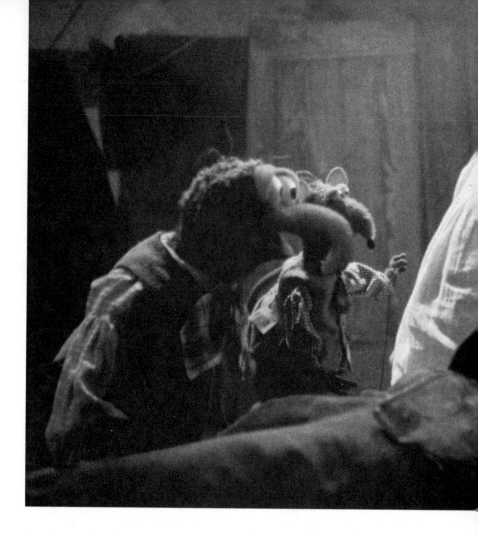

Suddenly, Billy Bones clutched his heart. His eyes bugged out. He fell backward.

"Is he dead?" Rizzo whispered.

"Almost," Billy groaned. Then he called for Jim. "Here. Take the map. I had it all along!" he said.

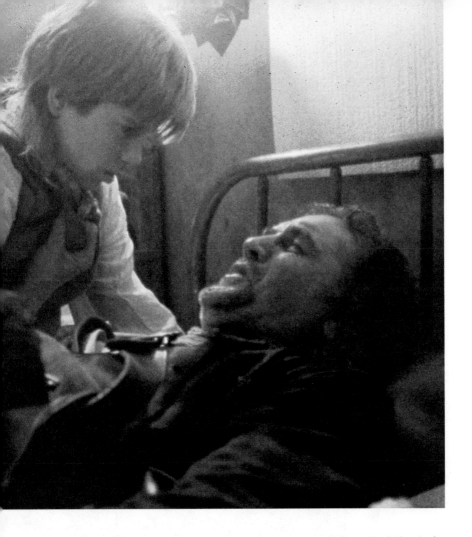

The map! Jim's eyes got wide. Did this mean there really <u>was</u> a treasure?

Billy Bones sat up again. "Beware the one-legged man!" Those were his last words.

Now he wasn't almost dead. He was really, really dead.

Jim, Gonzo, and Rizzo left the inn that very night. They were going to sail to the island—the island on the treasure map.

Jim found a ship. The captain was a dashing frog named Smollett.

But the crew was a strange and ugly
bunch. Most were missing something—a
hand, an eye, a head. And they smelled!
Did Jim care? Well…only when the wind
blew the wrong way.

By morning, the ship was on its way.
Jim was on his way, too—to find food! He
was starving. He followed his nose to the
galley. There, behind the counter, stood
the cook.

"I'm Long John Silver," he told Jim.
"Can I get you some grub, lad?"

"Grub sounds good." Jim nodded.

Long John handed Jim a dish of grub
stew. Jim tried a bite. Some of the grubs
were still moving. Yuck!

Long John smiled at Jim. "I'll get you
some swamp water to wash it down," he
said.

Long John grabbed a crutch from the wall. Thump! Thump! He came out from behind the counter. Jim stared at him.

Long John Silver had only one leg!

Was Long John the one-legged man Billy Bones had warned Jim about? No! He couldn't be. Long John was just a cook— a pretty bad cook. But he was no pirate!

Soon Long John and Jim became best friends. Long John taught Jim how to steer the ship. He taught Jim which star pointed north. And Jim told Long John everything. He even told him about the treasure map.

"Your secret is safe with me," Long John said.

But was Jim's secret really safe? Don't bet a piece of eight on it!

A few days later, Jim, Rizzo, and Gonzo were on deck. They heard some sailors talking.

"Guess what?" said one of the sailors.
"The boy had the treasure map. And I
stole it!"

Oh no! Jim knew that voice. It was Long John Silver! He wasn't just a rotten cook. He was a rotten pirate! The sailors were all pirates!

Just then a cry rang out. "Land Ho!" Someone had spotted the island.

Jim jumped up. He had to warn the
captain about the pirates. But Jim never
got the chance.

"Not so fast!" said Long John. He
grabbed Jim and pulled him into a boat.
The pirates were taking the boat to the
island.

"Cast away, men!" Long John shouted.

"'Bye, Jim." Rizzo waved from the deck. "Have a good time!"

Gonzo shook his head. "Cheese brain! Jim isn't going sightseeing," he said. "Jim is a prisoner!"

The pirates landed on the island. It was wild and overgrown—no motels, no fast food, no road even!

They hacked a trail through the jungle. They were looking for the treasure.

At last they came to a huge cave. Flint's treasure cave!

"The treasure is ours!" the pirates shouted with glee.

"No more swabbing decks!" cheered one.

"No more of Long John's cooking!" yelled another.

"Disney World, here we come!" they all shouted.

The pirates raced to the cave. It was
full of big sea chests. The pirates flung
open the chests one by one. But they all
had the same thing inside.

Nothing!

Now the pirates were mad. They turned on Long John.

"There's no treasure. And no...no... Disney World," sobbed Polly Lobster.

The pirates took out their knives. Long John Silver did not move.

"Run, lad," he whispered to Jim.
"Run for your life!"

Jim was surprised. Long John was no
angel. But he was not <u>all</u> bad!

"Run!" Long John said again.

Jim ran.

Jim was free. But the captain, Rizzo, and Gonzo did not know it. They sneaked onto the island to rescue Jim. Before long they heard a strange snuffling sound.

"Gonzo, do you have a cold?" Rizzo asked. "I have some nose spray."

But it was not Gonzo. It was five huge warty boars!

They grabbed the captain, Rizzo, and Gonzo and carried them off.

The boars took the prisoners to a clearing. Then the boars began to dance. "Boom-shakka-shakka-shakka! Boom-shakka-shakka-shakka!" the boars chanted.

Rizzo, Gonzo, and Smollett were scared. Was this the end?

All of a sudden, an elephant walked into the clearing. There was a big tent on its back. The tent flaps opened slowly. And out stepped—a jungle goddess! The Queen of the Boars!

The boars bowed low.

"Thank you. Thank you," said the queen. "I love you, too."

"Benjamina!" the captain cried. He knew this pig. She was not just a jungle goddess. She was his old girlfriend—his old ex-girlfriend, Benjamina Gunn.

The pig looked at the frog. "Smolly?" she asked. She was surprised. She was also mad. Really mad!

"You dumped me on our wedding day!" she shouted. "So take that!"

With a mighty "Hi-yaa!" she sent Smollett flying. He sailed across the clearing and right into a gong.

BOING!

Benjamina fixed her gloves and turned to the guards. She pointed at Gonzo and Rizzo.

"Tie them to the stake," she said. "But not him," she added. She grabbed the poor frog. "He comes with me!"

Jim had seen the whole thing. He sneaked up to the stake when the boars were not looking.

"Hey guys!" he whispered.

"Jim!" Rizzo and Gonzo cried. "Get us out of here."

One of the boars was cutting up carrots into a big pot of boiling water.

"The boars are having something new for dinner—" Gonzo said. "US!"

After Jim cut them loose, the three friends searched the island for the captain. Finally they spotted him with the pig queen...and Long John Silver.

Captain Smollet was hanging upside down over the edge of a cliff. So was the pig queen.

"For the last time, where is the treasure?" Long John hissed. He raised his sword to cut the captain's rope.

"Stop!" the pig queen shrieked. "Don't hurt my frog! The treasure is at my place!"

Treasure!

Long John flung open the door to the pig queen's house. There was Flint's treasure! Sparkling jewels! Gold coins! It was the real stuff, too, not chocolate money.

Suddenly the pirates appeared. Now
they all wanted to be Long John's best
friend.

"Long John, old buddy, old pal,"
Polly Lobster whined. "Need a hand,
hook, or claw?"

The pirates carried the treasure to the beach. They loaded it onto rowboats.

"When we tried to kill you, we were only kidding," the pirates told Long John.

The pirates were so busy, they did not see the big ship sailing toward them. Jim was at the helm. He was ready to take on the pirates. But first he had to save the captain—and that pig queen, too.

Jim peered through his spyglass. The ropes were about to break. There was not a moment to lose!

Jim sailed the ship right below Benjamina and Smollett. <u>Snap</u>! The ropes broke. The frog and the pig dropped down, down, down. They landed safely on the ship!

"It is about time you got here," Benjamina huffed.

Then all of a sudden, there was a sound like thunder. Two cannon balls soared through the air! Jim was firing at the pirates! The cannon balls smashed the rowboats. Pirates scattered everywhere.

After that, it did not take long to capture the pirates. The captain locked them up. Then he loaded the treasure and set sail for home, where they all lived happily...

Wait! Stop! That's not the end. Not quite. We can't forget about Long John! The ship's jail did not hold him for long. He found a way out. He stole two large treasure chests and one small boat.

Jim watched the pirate sneak away. He did not try to stop Long John. Long John was not all bad. And besides... he had stolen a leaky boat.

Soon the sun sank into the sea. And so did Long John's boat.

And what about Long John Silver? He was stuck on Treasure Island—forever!

THE END

(Really!)